Scheherezade Children's Stories

The
Magic Lamp

GARNET PUBLISHING LIMITED

Translation from Arabic Copyright © 1993 Garnet Publishing

First English Edition

ISBN I 873938 92 6

British Library Cataloguing-in-Publication Data.
A catalogue record for this book is available from the British Library.

Edited by Katherine Judge
Text Design by David Rose
Typeset by Samantha Abley
Printed in Lebanon

Published by
Garnet Publishing Ltd, 8 Southern Court, South Street, Reading RGI 4QS, UK.

One day Aladdin caught sight of the emperor's beautiful daughter outside his house. He was so overcome by her beauty that he decided to ask her to marry him.

The next morning he went to see the emperor and asked his permission to marry her.

'I agree to give you my daughter's hand in marriage,' the emperor replied, 'provided that, in return, you bring me forty glasses filled with precious stones.'

Aladdin rubbed his magic lamp and immediately the jewels appeared before him.

He presented them to the emperor who at once consented and the couple were married with great pomp and ceremony.

A little while later, Aladdin left the palace one morning to go hunting. While he was away a beggar came to the door and offered the princess a new lamp for her old one. The princess, who did not know about the lamp's magic powers, gladly exchanged it for a new one.

The beggar was, in fact, a magician in disguise and at once he called upon the genie of the lamp to carry the princess to his castle so that she could be his slave.

When Aladdin came home he realised what had happened. He travelled through many lands and searched for many years until at last he found his beloved wife in the magician's castle. He quickly gave the princess a magic potion and told her to put it in the magician's wine glass.

That evening, when the magician returned, the princess gave him his glass of wine. As he drank it he fell into a deep sleep and as he did so, Aladdin crept into the room and got his lamp. Immediately he rubbed it and when the genie appeared he commanded it to take them back to their own home.

When they arrived at the palace Aladdin threw the lamp into the sea to be rid of its curse and the couple lived happily ever after.